Word List

Here is a list of words that might make it easier to read this book. You'll find them in boldface the first time they appear in the story.

serious	SEAR-ee-uhs
dedicated	DE-di-kayt-tid
unison	YOO-nuh-suhn
business	BIZ-nuhs
categories	CA-tuh-gor-eez
focusing	FOH-kuhs-ing
rummaging	RUH-mij-ing
machine	muh-SHEEN
receipts	ri-SEETS
schedule	SKE-juhl
headache	HE-dayk
thermometer	thuh-MO-muh-ter
contagious	kuhn-TAY-juhs
customers	KUHS-tuh-mers

Barbie™

Little Sisters Keep Out

Published by Grolier Books, a division of Grolier Enterprises, Inc. Story by Linda Williams Aber. Photo crew: Dennis Di Laura, Barb Miller, Robert Guillaume, Shirley Ushirogata, and Lisa Collins. Produced by Bumpy Slide Books.
Printed in the United States of America.
ISBN: 0-7172-8855-2

GROLIER
B O O K S

Chapter One

"Okay, you three," Stacie said to her giggling friends. "As president of the Best Friends' Club, I now call our first meeting to order."

Stacie looked around her room and nodded at each of the girls. Katie rested comfortably in the beanbag chair. She was chatting with Janet, who sat on the floor. Whitney sat on the bed, waiting for the meeting to begin. Stacie stood by her desk, looking very much like a club president.

Pushing her blond bangs out of her eyes, Stacie glanced down at the yellow pad in her hand. It read, *Best Friends' Club Meeting*. Tapping her purple pen on the edge of the pad, Stacie tried again. "Order!" she called out. "Order in the bedroom! We've got work to do!"

"Work!" Whitney exclaimed. "I thought we were supposed to be having fun!"

Stacie explained, "The work we have to do is to plan our fun, Silly!"

"Right," Janet agreed. "Half the fun of having fun is planning it!"

Now even Stacie had to laugh. When she and her best friends got together, it was almost impossible to be **serious.** But Stacie really wanted this club to work. The last club they had tried to start had quickly fallen apart.

The previous fall, the girls had formed the Super Clue Club. The club was **dedicated** to solving mysteries. But after two weeks, the biggest mystery they had had to solve was finding a mystery! It seemed as if nobody in their neighborhood had ever lost anything bigger than a button.

One day, a mysterious package had arrived in Katie's mailbox. It was addressed to her, but there was no return address. The girls were excited. They thought they had a real mystery to solve at last!

But the package turned out to be from the Puff Puffs Cereal Company. Inside the package was a pink plastic watch. Katie had forgotten that six weeks earlier, she'd sent away two box tops to get the watch. Mystery solved!

After that, the friends took a break from club stuff for a while. But now that it was summer, starting a new club seemed like a great idea.

Stacie tried again to call the meeting to order. "We have important things to talk about," she said over the girls' laughter. "We have to plan a club event that will make lots of money."

"Money?" Janet, Katie, and Whitney asked together. The three girls sat up taller and gave Stacie their full attention.

"Yes," Stacie answered. "This time, let's be a club that really does something important. The Community Center is trying to raise money to buy new playground equipment. If we plan a club activity that earns money, we can help buy new swings."

"That's a great idea!" Katie said.

Then Whitney spoke up. "But how will we make money?" she asked.

"How about starting a neighborhood dog-walking service?" Janet suggested.

"That's a good idea," Stacie replied.

"But don't you have the only dog in the neighborhood?" Whitney asked.

"Hmmm," Janet replied, "I guess you're right. And I suppose nobody's going to pay me to walk my own dog."

"I know!" Katie cried. "What about having a Bike Wash Day? We could wash bicycles and charge money for it!"

"That's not bad," Whitney said. "Or how about . . . ummm . . . "

All four girls were silent as they tried to think of other ways to make money. After a few moments, they all started talking at once.

"I know!" Janet cried.

"How about . . . ," Whitney began.

"A sale?" Katie started.

"A *toy* sale!" Stacie, Katie, Janet, and Whitney shouted in **unison.**

"Great minds think alike," Stacie laughed.

"It must be a good idea if we all thought of it!" added Janet.

Four hands flew out to give high fives.

5

"Congratulations! We did it!" Whitney cried.

Now it was time to get down to **business** and plan the big event.

Stacie wrote *Toy Sale* on her pad. She started to list what they had to do to get ready. "We'll need to collect all our old toys," she began.

Whitney added,"We want to make sure they're clean and in good condition."

"And we should probably make sure it's okay with our families," Katie said.

Everyone agreed.

Stacie was happy. The first meeting of the Best Friends' Club was getting off to a great start. "We'll have **categories,**" she continued. "Games, dolls, puzzles, stuffed animals, and—"

Just as Stacie was about to say "books," the door to her room flew open. In walked her baby sister, Kelly. Kelly had applesauce all over her cheeks and hands. The giggling toddler ran over to Whitney and threw herself onto her lap.

"Kelly play, too!" she said. "Kelly play, too!"

Whitney reached behind her and grabbed a tissue from the box on the bedside table. She wiped Kelly's hands and face and tickled her clean cheek. "You silly little girl!" Whitney told her playfully.

"Let me hold her!" Katie said, reaching over from the beanbag chair.

Kelly climbed over Janet to Katie. Suddenly all the girls' attention was on Kelly. Whitney, Janet, and Katie took turns playing peekaboo, patty-cake, and "How Big Is Kelly?" with her.

At first, Stacie laughed at her cute baby sister. But as the games went on and on, she started wishing her friends would get back to **focusing** on the club's business.

Nobody was paying attention to the plans they had made. What about the toy sale? What about making money to buy swings? All anyone seemed to care about was Kelly. Her friends were having more fun with the toddler than with Stacie. And Stacie wasn't having any fun at all.

Stacie felt funny inside. There was a knot in her stomach and another knot in her throat. Her eyes filled up with tears. She had been feeling funny a lot lately, especially when her little sister was around.

Chapter Two

For the rest of the meeting, Stacie was quieter than usual. But nobody seemed to notice. She guessed that her friends would have played with Kelly forever if Nellie, the cat, hadn't joined the meeting, too. The cat had wandered into the room, and Kelly had chased her out of the room and down the hall.

With her little sister gone, Stacie was finally able to bring the meeting back to order. Before it was time for Katie, Janet, and Whitney to leave, they had finished planning the toy sale. They had decided that each of them would donate her old toys and games. They had planned to bring the items over to Stacie's house and put prices on them at the next club meeting.

After her friends left, Stacie began **rummaging** through the basement. She couldn't believe how much old stuff was down there. Deciding what to sell and what to keep was not as easy as she'd thought it would be. Each toy held a loving memory for her.

Stacie began putting toys into an empty box. She started with an old tea set, some colorful balls, plastic food, and a toy shopping cart. Then she gathered up jigsaw puzzles, books, an old snow cone **machine,** some board games, and an unused set of watercolors. Last of all, Stacie found a very special old toy. It was her stuffed cat, Cookie.

When Stacie was two years old, she had carried Cookie everywhere. Cookie was her favorite cuddly toy. But when she had started

OLD
TOYS

school, Stacie had left Cookie behind. Pretty soon she was interested in other toys and games. So Cookie had gone to live in the basement.

"Well," Stacie said, carefully examining Cookie, "I guess keeping you down here was a good idea. You look just the way I remember you!"

Cookie's pretty patchwork was a little faded, but her blue eyes were perfect. The little pink, embroidered mouth smiled sweetly up at Stacie. She tipped Cookie over to look at her paws.

"Meow!" the cat cried.

Stacie turned Cookie over again and again.

"Meow! Meow! Meow!" the soft toy repeated.

Holding Cookie, Stacie remembered when she had been the youngest one in the family, before Kelly was born. Stacie could recall the day Kelly had been brought home from the hospital.

* * * *

Stacie and her oldest sister, Barbie, were fixing up Kelly's room. They hung pictures on the wall and placed baby rattles and toys on top of the dresser. As the sisters worked side by side to make the room cozy and comfortable for Kelly, Barbie talked about how much fun it was to be a big sister.

"Like you are to me?" Stacie asked.

"Exactly," Barbie replied. She patted Stacie's blond curls and started fixing the curtains.

Suddenly Stacie ran to her room and came back with her stuffed kitten, Cookie. She placed Cookie on the rocking chair in the baby's room. Stacie stared at it for a minute. She had thought it would be nice to give her favorite toy to the new baby. But when she looked at Cookie sitting on the chair, Stacie felt sad.

Barbie saw the worried look on Stacie's little face. She stopped what she was doing and kneeled down in front of Stacie. Barbie hugged her tightly. Stacie buried her face in Barbie's shoulder.

"Don't worry, Stacie," Barbie whispered.

"You'll be a great big sister."

Stacie wasn't sure how to tell Barbie the real reason she felt sad.

Barbie then took one last look around the room before giving Stacie's shoulder a gentle squeeze. "There!" Barbie said. "Baby Kelly's room is ready. Are you?"

"I guess so," Stacie answered slowly.

Barbie and Stacie left the room together. But Stacie was having second thoughts about giving away Cookie.

Later that day, while everyone was busy with the new baby, Stacie walked back into her little sister's room and took Cookie off the chair.

* * * *

That had happened almost two years before. Now, as she held her old toy in her hands, Stacie was surprised at how much she remembered.

Just then the phone rang upstairs.

"Stacie?" Barbie called down the basement

stairs. "Whitney's calling for you!"

"I'll be right there," Stacie yelled back. She placed Cookie in the box of toys for the sale.

As she ran upstairs, Stacie heard a soft "Meow!" coming from the basement.

Chapter Three

Whitney's phone call was about the next day's surprise.

"What surprise?" Stacie asked her friend.

"Barbie invited Katie, Janet, and me to go shopping with you," Whitney explained.

When Stacie hung up, Barbie stood in the doorway, smiling. "Oh, well. Skipper and I had wanted to surprise you. We remember when we started our own clubs," she said. "Now that you're starting one, we want to take you and your friends shopping for club supplies tomorrow."

"Yippee!" Stacie shouted. This was just the

news she needed to get her mind off Kelly. She hugged Barbie and ran to her room to make a list.

The next day, Whitney, Janet, and Katie arrived early. "We're here!" they called from the front porch of Stacie's house. The day was just beginning, but they were already giggling.

"Come in!" Stacie said.

"No, you come out!" Janet called, laughing.

"Yes, let's head out," Barbie added, greeting the girls at the front door. "We have shopping to do!"

"I tried to make a list," Stacie said, "but I wasn't really sure what we needed."

"Let's see what you have. 'Clipboards, colored markers, paper, stickers,'" Barbie read out loud. "That's good. If you're going to have a toy sale, you'll need to make signs and hang them up around the neighborhood."

"And you'll need to put prices on everything," Skipper added.

"You'll also want to give **receipts** to people who buy things," Barbie continued.

Barbie's friend Midge had agreed to baby-sit Kelly while everyone was out shopping. The store was a short walk from the house. Barbie and Skipper led the way. Stacie and her friends followed close behind. But before they had gotten very far, they heard a voice calling out, "Kelly come, too! Kelly come, too!"

The girls turned and looked up the street. There was Kelly, followed closely by Midge. Kelly's blond head bounced merrily as she ran to catch up with the group.

"Oh, no!" Stacie moaned.

"That's okay," Whitney said. "We can watch her."

"If she gets tired of walking, we'll take turns carrying her," Katie added.

"Kelly come, too!" Kelly said with a big smile, catching up to them.

Midge turned to Barbie and said, "For a little girl, she sure is fast!" Then she reached for Kelly's hand and said, "Let's go home, little one."

Barbie looked at Stacie and asked, "Do you mind if she comes, Stacie?"

"I guess not," Stacie replied slowly.

Barbie reached down for Kelly. "Okay, Kelly. You can come, too."

"We'll just bring her along. Thanks for your help, Midge. See you later," Barbie told her friend.

"Yay!" Kelly cheered, clapping her hands.

The girls laughed and told Kelly how cute she was. Stacie didn't say a word. She tried to smile and look happy. "Oh, well," she thought. "At least we're still going shopping."

The girls took turns holding Kelly's hands and swinging her as they walked. They came to a park halfway between home and the store.

Kelly ran to the playground area. "Swing me!" she cried.

One regular swing and one baby swing were the only two left on the swing set. The other two swings were broken. The seats were gone, and their chains dangled loosely.

Stacie pointed to the broken swings. "See?" she said to her friends. "Our club is going to earn some money to help get new swings. Won't that be great?"

"Swing me!" Kelly repeated. The other girls didn't say anything about the sale. Instead, they all turned their attention to Kelly. Suddenly the club-shopping trip became the play-with-Kelly trip.

"Okay, we'll swing you," Katie said. She lifted Kelly up and put her in the swing. Katie told the toddler to hold on tightly. Stepping behind the swing, she gave it a gentle push.

"Wheee!" Kelly cried, kicking her feet.

All the girls took turns pushing her. When Kelly wanted to get down and try the slide, Stacie's friends followed happily.

"Aren't the girls great with Kelly?" Skipper asked Barbie.

"Kelly sure is happy, isn't she?" Barbie said.

"That gives me an idea," Skipper said suddenly. "Maybe the girls will help us plan Kelly's birthday party."

Whitney overheard Skipper talking to Barbie. "That's a great idea!" she squealed. "We'd love to help! It could be a club project! When is the party?"

"In two Saturdays," Skipper said. "We'll have plenty of time to plan if we start right away."

All the talk turned to the party. Suddenly Stacie realized that the party was going to be on the very same day as the club's toy sale!

"Wait a minute," Stacie began. "That's the day we're—"

Before she could finish her sentence, Janet, Katie, and Whitney were bubbling over with ideas for Kelly's party.

Stacie hated to admit it, but that funny

feeling was back. Once again, Kelly was cutting into all her plans.

Stacie's friends got so involved in the party plans, they almost forgot about shopping!

"Hey," Stacie reminded them, "what about our shopping trip?"

"Yes," Barbie said. "We'd better get going. It's almost time for lunch!"

As they were leaving the park, Kelly ran over to the sandbox. She climbed in and busily began patting the piles of sand with her hands.

"Time to go, Kelly," Stacie called to her.

Kelly stood up and tumbled forward into the sand. "Ow!" she screamed, rubbing her eyes with her sandy hands. Big tears rolled down her chubby cheeks.

Barbie ran over to her. Cupping her hands, Katie carried water from the water fountain over to Kelly. Barbie took a tissue from her pocket and dipped it into the water. She gently wiped the sand from Kelly's eyes. Soon Kelly calmed down, but she began to yawn.

"Kelly go home," she said.

Even Stacie could see that Kelly was too tired to go shopping. She needed a nap. They would have to go home.

"I'm sorry," Barbie said. She put an arm around Stacie and squeezed her shoulder. "I know how disappointed you are. We'll go shopping tomorrow. I promise."

Stacie was more than disappointed. She was angry and sad. Stacie tried to push her feelings away. "Oh, well," she told herself. "Tomorrow we'll start getting ready for the toy sale. The toy sale is going to be great . . . if my friends remember to come!"

Chapter Four

The next day, Stacie sat alone in the kitchen putting price tags on the toys in front of her. She could hear Whitney, Janet, and Katie talking with Skipper in the backyard. Stacie's friends had come over early because there was so much to do.

Every once in a while, through the open window, she heard Skipper say things like, "Kelly will love that!" and "That will be perfect for Kelly's friends."

Stacie's friends were busy planning Kelly's second birthday party while Stacie worked on the toy sale by herself. Whitney and the other girls had gathered their old toys and brought them to Stacie's house. But instead of making price tags and setting up tables, her friends were choosing games for Kelly's party.

"Hey!" Stacie called out the window to the girls. "Aren't you going to help me?"

"We will," Whitney replied. "But first come out and help us plan the party. We need you!"

"No, thanks," Stacie replied. Then she tried again to turn her friends' attention away from Kelly's party. She suggested doing things she knew Kelly wouldn't be able to do. "I found an old hula hoop in the box!" Stacie cried. "Let's have a hula hoop contest and see who wins!"

"Maybe later," Janet said.

"Anyone want to ride bikes around the neighborhood?" Stacie asked next.

"That would be fun," Katie answered. "But let's do it later."

"I know," Stacie tried again. "Let's climb

trees and spy on the pesky boys next door!" She knew they all loved to do that! Surely that would break up the party planning.

"The boys went away for a few days," Skipper reminded Stacie. "And spying isn't very nice, anyway."

Stacie was just about to give up. Before her friends arrived, she had made up a **schedule** for their club meeting. She looked over her list and sighed.

Things to Do

1. Sort the toys.
2. Make price tags.
3. Set up tables in the garage.
4. Organize toys on the tables.
5. Eat ice pops.

"Ice pops!" Stacie remembered. "That should get their attention!"

Stacie put her list aside and hurried to the refrigerator. Reaching inside the freezer, she pulled out a box of ice pops.

"Hey, you guys!" Stacie called out the kitchen door. "Ice pop time!"

That did it! Whitney, Katie, Janet, Skipper, and even Kelly lined up at the door for an ice pop. The girls eagerly gobbled up the icy treats.

But soon everyone was giggling over Kelly's face. It had turned blue from the melting ice pop.

Stacie finally gave up. Since her friends were more interested in Kelly than in the toy sale, Stacie decided she would just have to set things up all by herself.

While the others played with her little sister, Stacie went to work.

When Barbie came home, she offered to

take Stacie shopping for club supplies. But Stacie said that she didn't feel like going.

By the end of the afternoon, Stacie was feeling sad and lonely. She also had a terrible **headache.**

When Barbie peeked in the kitchen to see how Stacie was doing, she was surprised. Stacie was looking red and flushed. Barbie felt Stacie's forehead. Then she got out the **thermometer** and took Stacie's temperature.

"A hundred and one degrees," Barbie said, reading the thermometer. "I thought you felt warm."

Barbie took Stacie's face in her hands and looked into her eyes. They looked red. Then she glanced at Stacie's arm and saw three red dots in a row.

"Chicken pox!" Barbie exclaimed. "That explains why you haven't been yourself lately."

"Chicken pox!" Stacie moaned. "But what about the toy sale?"

"Right now, we've got to get you into bed," Barbie said kindly. "Whitney and Janet have already had chicken pox. But Katie and Kelly haven't. You're **contagious.**"

"Contagious?" asked Stacie.

"Yes," replied Barbie. "That means someone who hasn't had the chicken pox yet could catch it from you."

"I don't feel well," Stacie said, leaning against Barbie.

"I know," Barbie said, stroking Stacie's hair. "You'll feel better in a few days," Barbie continued, leading Stacie up to her room. "You should try to sleep now. I'll tell your friends you'll talk to them later."

Stacie crawled between her cool sheets. Barbie placed a glass of water on Stacie's bedside table and left her to sleep.

Lying in bed, Stacie remembered what Barbie had said about her not being herself lately.

As she drifted off to sleep, Stacie thought about the way she had been feeling lately. What Barbie had said was very true. She wasn't herself at all. She felt miserable, inside and out.

Chapter Five

"Chicken pox!" Katie, Whitney, and Janet exclaimed when they heard the news.

"That must be why she's been so quiet lately," Whitney said.

"We'll take care of everything," Janet declared. "She'll be better by the day of the birthday party."

"And the toy sale!" Katie added.

The girls called Stacie every day. Janet and Whitney had already had the chicken pox. So they were allowed to deliver get-well cards and balloons to their friend. But Stacie wasn't very good company during their visits. By the third day, Stacie had decided not to have any more visitors for a while. She didn't want anyone to see her covered from head to toe in red bumps.

By the end of the following week, Stacie's itchy red dots were drying up. One morning she lay in bed holding a mirror up to her face. "Ugh!" she moaned. "Go away, dumb spots!" she cried. Stacie was no longer contagious, but her face was still covered with spots.

Suddenly there was a knock on her door. "Who is it?" she asked, putting the mirror down.

"It's me," Barbie answered. "May I come in?"

"I guess so," Stacie said. "If you don't mind looking at my polka-dotted face."

The door opened, and Barbie came in. She held her hands behind her back. "I have a surprise for you," she said.

Stacie's eyes lit up. "You do?" she said.

Barbie sat on the edge of Stacie's bed. "Ta da!" she sang out, handing her sister a package in clear wrapping. "For your club!"

Stacie sat up and took the package from Barbie. She peeked through the clear wrapper and squealed with delight. "Wow!" she cried, tearing open the paper.

Inside was a sparkly, purple clipboard with

 her name at the top! Clipped to the board were sheets of colored paper, stickers, and markers.

"Skipper and I got one for each of your club members," Barbie explained.

Stacie spread the stickers, papers, and markers out on her lap. Then she saw the note from Barbie clipped to the board. "You'll always be my baby sister," Stacie read silently.

Tears formed in Stacie's eyes. "Thank you," she whispered to Barbie. "I'm sorry I've been so grumpy lately."

"Well," Barbie said, "chicken pox can make a person feel pretty bad."

Stacie thought for a moment and then spoke slowly. "It wasn't just the chicken pox," she explained. "It was something much worse: the jealous pox."

"Oh?" Barbie said softly, tipping her head to one side. "I knew that something was up, but I thought it was because you were getting sick. I didn't realize you were feeling that way."

"I was feeling awful," Stacie said sadly. "Until I got the chicken pox, my friends were paying more attention to Kelly than they were to me. It feels like that always happens, because Kelly is so cute. Just like when . . ."

"Just like when baby Kelly first came home from the hospital," Barbie said.

"Yes," Stacie answered. "The club meetings, the shopping trip, and the toy sale all got pushed aside by Kelly's party. My own friends were more interested in my baby sister than they were in me."

Barbie put a comforting arm around Stacie's shoulder. "Stacie," she said softly, "everybody feels jealous sometimes."

"Even you?" Stacie gasped.

Barbie laughed. "Sure! I remember how I felt when Skipper was the new baby and *I* was the big sister. Part of me felt so happy to have a new baby sister. But another part of me felt sad and a little jealous because I wasn't the baby anymore. But one day, when Skipper was just learning to talk, she said to me, 'Barbie help Skipper?' She wanted me to help her climb up onto a chair. In fact, she always wanted me to be the one to help her do things. And that made me feel good. Pretty soon I began to see how important a big sister was."

"And still is," Stacie said, giving Barbie a hug.

"And little sisters are important, too," Barbie

went on. "Families and clubs are a lot alike," she said. "Each member is important to the whole group. All the time you've been sick, our family has felt as if an important piece were missing."

"Do you think my friends in the club feel that way, too?" Stacie asked.

"I'm sure of it," Barbie replied.

Just then there was another knock at the door. The door opened slowly. It was Kelly, holding out her baby cup of juice. "Juice!" Kelly said. "Juice for Stacie!"

Stacie took the cup and pretended to drink. Kelly patted Stacie's hand. "Feel better, Stacie," she said.

Stacie couldn't help giggling at Kelly's expression. It felt good to laugh again.

Chapter Six

Finally it was the day of the club's toy sale.

Stacie couldn't believe her eyes when Whitney, Katie, and Janet led her to the garage. "Wow!" she gasped. "You really did take care of everything!"

All the toys, books, and games sat sorted, tagged, and ready on long tables.

"We told you not to worry," Whitney laughed. "We planned to have the toy sale in the morning."

"And Kelly's birthday party in the afternoon," Katie added.

"You didn't think we were going to let a

41

bunch of red spots ruin all of our plans, did you?"
said Janet.

"Thanks, you guys," replied Stacie.

She looked over the selection of sale items.
In the middle of the bears, lions, and dogs on the
stuffed-animals end of the table was Stacie's old
favorite, Cookie.

"So what do you think?" Whitney asked.

"I think you're the best friends anyone could
have!" Stacie exclaimed. "And I think our toy sale
is going to be great!" She looked at the clock.
"People should start coming any time now."

Janet took her place behind the dolls. Whitney
did some last-minute arranging and then stood over
by the books. Katie headed for the games.
Stacie took charge of the stuffed animals.

The neighborhood signs had paid off. People
were already starting to arrive.

"Look!" Janet cried.

"Here come our first **customers**!" Katie added.

All morning the four friends helped people pick out just the right toys to buy. They sold a red wagon and the plastic kitchen set with the plastic food. Two boys bought all the sports books. A grandmother and granddaughter bought a few board games, a checkers set, and two jigsaw puzzles.

While Barbie helped Stacie collect the money, Whitney and Katie put things in bags and wrote out receipts. Janet kept the tables looking neat and tidy. Making money to help buy swings for the playground was fun. But working together was the most fun of all.

Just before noon, Stacie saw three little girls walking up the driveway. She recognized them as the Johnson triplets from up the street: Anna, Eva, and Emma. Except for their hairstyles, they looked exactly alike. Anna's hair was tied up in a ponytail. Eva wore her hair short. Emma's hair was curly. They all looked like serious shoppers.

43

BOOKS
for
SALE

DOLLS

GAMES

Each of them carried a clear plastic purse with coins inside.

"Hello," Anna said, her ponytail bouncing. "Do you have any mystery books?"

"Right over here," Whitney replied. "We have all kinds of books to choose from."

"May I help you?" Stacie asked Eva and Emma.

"We just want to look first," answered Eva.

"Take your time," Stacie said politely. "There's plenty of good stuff left."

Stacie and her friends watched the three sisters walk from table to table. Anna, Eva, and Emma looked things over carefully.

"Oh!" Anna exclaimed suddenly. "How cute!" She leaned across the table, pointing to Cookie. Then Anna reached over and picked up the cuddly toy.

"Meow!" Cookie cried.

"We have lots of other stuffed animals,"

Stacie said quickly. She picked up a bear in one hand and a lion in the other.

"But this one talks!" Anna replied. She tipped Cookie over again and again. Cookie's "meow" echoed through the garage.

Eva and Emma gathered around to see what was making all the noise. "Are you going to buy the kitty, Anna?" Eva asked, patting Cookie.

"I have to think about it," Anna answered. "She is cute, but look at this poor bear!"

Anna put Cookie back on the pile and picked up a raggedy blue bear with pink paws. One of the bear's eyes was missing, so he looked like he was always winking. "This one is so sweet," Anna said, hugging the bear. Then she turned back to Cookie. Anna stood holding Cookie in one arm and the bear in the other.

Stacie could tell that Anna was having trouble deciding between them. Seeing Anna holding the bear didn't bother Stacie. But seeing her holding Cookie did.

In her mind, Stacie pictured Cookie sitting on Anna's bed. She imagined Anna falling asleep with Cookie curled in her arms. Suddenly Stacie felt a familiar knot in her stomach. "Do I really want to sell Cookie?" she asked herself.

"The bear is really sweet," Stacie said to Anna. She was hoping the girl would forget about Cookie.

Anna took a closer look at Cookie and the bear. Cookie meowed. The bear winked.

"I don't know what to do!" Anna cried.

Stacie made a quick decision. Reaching across the table, she plucked Cookie from Anna's arms. "I'm sorry," Stacie said. "I think I made a big mistake. This stuffed animal isn't for sale."

"Oh!" Anna exclaimed. "Then I'll just take

the bear, please."

Stacie breathed a big sigh of relief. "You will?" she said. "Great! Let me put him in a bag for you."

While Anna counted out three coins, Stacie carefully put the bear into a bag. Then she took Cookie off the table and hid the cat in a corner under her sweatshirt.

"Shhh!" she whispered to Cookie as she laid her down.

It looked as if the three sisters were going to be the last customers of the day.

"You're in luck!" Stacie said to them. "Everything that's left just went on sale. It's three for the price of one now!" She handed the stuffed lion to Eva and the dog to Emma.

Now all the stuffed animals were gone. The sisters did some last-minute shopping. They picked up three books and three decks of cards.

"Thanks!" they all shouted as Whitney

handed them receipts.

"We'll be back if you have another toy sale," Anna said, hugging her new bear.

As the three sisters skipped down the driveway, Stacie and her friends started cleaning up. They counted the money they had earned and declared the toy sale a big success.

"We definitely made enough to help the Community Center buy at least one new swing for the playground!" Stacie exclaimed.

"Hooray!" the others cheered.

"And there's even some money left to treat ourselves to ice cream at our next club event!" Stacie added

"Oh, my! The party!" Katie gasped. "That's our next club event!"

There was just enough time to put the tables away before Kelly's birthday party guests began arriving. Barbie and Skipper were already in the backyard waiting to greet Kelly's friends. They had spent the morning decorating, blowing up balloons, and putting the finishing touches on a birthday cake for Kelly. Barbie's friend Ken and his little brother Tommy had come over to help them set things up.

Skipper lifted Kelly up so she could see her cake.

"Yum-yum!" Kelly shouted excitedly. Katie, Whitney, and Janet laughed. So did Stacie.

While Stacie and her friends played games with Kelly's friends, Skipper took some pictures. Squeals of laughter filled the air as the little boys and girls chased balloons around the yard. Stacie looked around at the party scene and felt happy. Everybody was having a wonderful time. For the first time, Stacie realized how important each and every one of her friends and her sisters were to her. Together, they had made a great party.

After the last game was played, the birthday cake was eaten, and the presents were opened, Stacie had one more surprise. "Here, Kelly," she said. "This is my special present to you." She handed her baby sister a package wrapped in purple paper.

Kelly tore open the wrapping and squealed with glee. "Kitty!" she cried. "Pretty kitty!"

"Her name is Cookie," Stacie said. "She used to be my toy. Now I want you to have her."

Kelly hugged Cookie with one arm and Stacie with the other.

Barbie put her arm around Stacie, too. "You're a good big sister," she whispered to Stacie. "I'm very proud of you."

Stacie smiled happily. It had been a perfect day. "I had a good teacher," she replied, looking at her oldest sister. "Happy birthday, Baby Kelly!"

"Kelly not baby," Kelly replied, holding Cookie up above her head. "Kelly two!"

Laughter filled the air as everybody clapped and cheered for Kelly.

Everyone except Cookie, who just said, "Meow!"